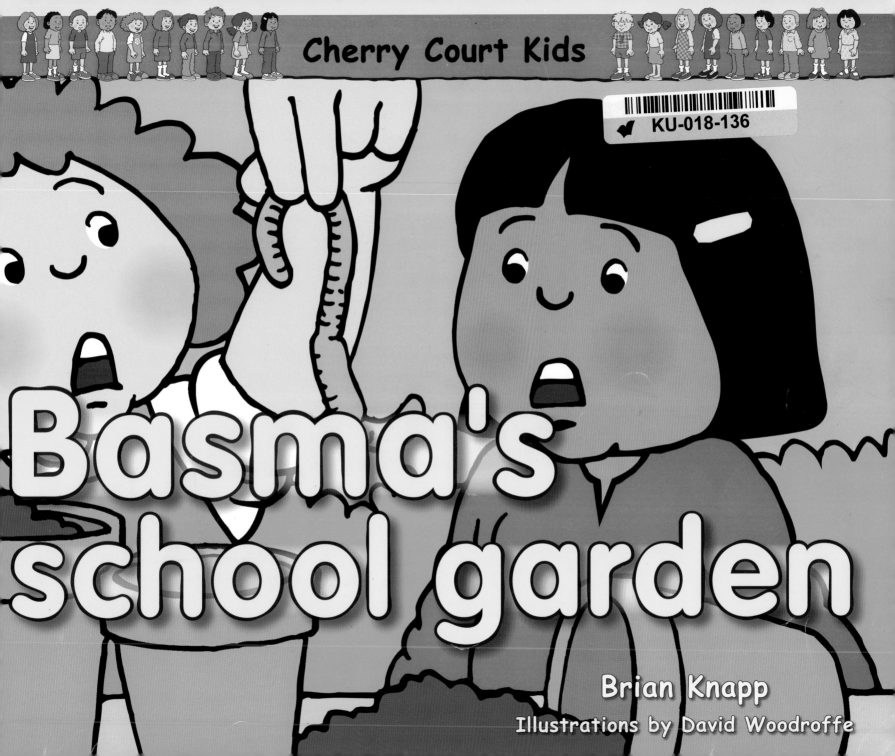

Basma's school garden

Brian Knapp

Illustrations by David Woodroffe

A (Curriculum Visions) Citizenship book from Atlantic Europe Publishing

Teacher's Resources

There is a teacher's resource to accompany this book, available only from the publisher. Resources include photocopiable worksheets, lesson plans and curriculum correlation.

Cherry Court Kids CD-Rom

A CD-Rom featuring all six of the Cherry Court Kids is available only from the publisher.

Dedicated Web Site

There's more about other great Curriculum Visions packs and a wealth of supporting information available at our dedicated web site:

www.CurriculumVisions.com

Atlantic Europe Publishing

First published in 2003 by Atlantic Europe Publishing Company Ltd

Copyright © 2003 Atlantic Europe Publishing Company Ltd

This product is manufactured from sustainable managed forests. For every tree cut down at least one more is planted.

Author
Brian Knapp, BSc, PhD

Art Director
Duncan McCrae, BSc

Illustrator
David Woodroffe

Editor
Gillian Gatehouse

Senior Designer
Adele Humphries, BA

Acknowledgements
The publishers would like to thank *Kezia Humphries* and *Pauline Whitehouse* for their help and advice.

Designed and produced by
Earthscape Editions

Printed in Hong Kong by
Wing King Tong

Basma's school garden – Curriculum Visions
A CIP record for this book is available from the British Library

Paperback ISBN 186214 339 0
Hardback ISBN 186214 341 2

Contents

Basma has been to a city farm.

Basma visits a farm

Basma has just been to visit a city farm. It was a lovely day out.

While she was at the farm she was told that many schools have their own gardens.

Now Basma wants to start a garden in her own school. What should Basma do?

Choose what Basma should do:

① Suggest to the teacher that they need a school garden.

② Tell other children about how much fun it could be.

③ Forget about it because it would be a lot of effort.

or...

④ Can you think of something else?

What seeds shall we plant?

Seed time

It's spring and time to plant seeds.

Peter wants to plant flower seeds.

Su Yin wants to plant seeds for food.

Basma wants seeds that flower in spring, and Peter wants seeds that flower in summer.

What should they do?

Choose what the children should do:

① Plant all of what Peter wants.

② Plant some of each type of seed.

③ Ask the teacher to decide.

or...

④ Can you think of something else?

7

Basma finds Lisa sulking in a corner.

I don't want to join in!

Basma's friend Lisa is sitting sulking in a corner.

She says she hates gardens and doesn't see why she should plant silly seeds.

Everyone else is going to join in.

What should Basma do?

Choose what Basma should do:

1. Leave her to sit and sulk.

2. Force her to join in.

3. Try to get her to join in by asking if there is something she likes, such as smelling flowers.

or...

4. Can you think of something else?

9

Basma finds caterpillars eating the school plants.

The plants are being eaten

It has been a good spring and the seeds have sprouted well.

Then, one day, furry caterpillars are seen eating the plants. Basma knows that there are pest killers but she doesn't like killing things. What should Basma do?

Choose what Basma should do:

① Leave the caterpillars to eat the plants.

② Get her teacher to spray pest killer.

③ Pick the caterpillars off one by one and put them somewhere else.

or...

④ Can you think of something else?

Hard work is spoiled.

Thoughtless footprints

Basma and her friends are out in the garden.

They have just finished making it tidy when some boys run right across the garden and leave footprints in the soil.

What should Basma do?

Choose what Basma should do:

① Tell her teacher.

② Find the boys and tell them off.

③ Tidy up the garden and say nothing.

or...

④ Can you think of something else?

13

Emma and Basma find a worm.

Creepy crawlies

Basma's friend Emma has agreed to help empty the soil from the school flowerpots.

Suddenly Emma squeals because she has caught hold of a cold wriggly worm.

Emma drops the worm on the floor. What should Basma do?

Choose what Basma should do:

① Put the worm in a dustbin.

② Tell Emma that it is a living thing and must be returned carefully to the garden.

③ Scream and run to the teacher.

or...

④ Can you think of something else?

Everyone has lunch after working in the school garden.

Soiled fingers

Everyone has been helping to tidy up the school garden.

Suddenly it's lunch-time. Some children begin eating without washing their hands. They tell Basma that soil is natural and healthy.

What should Basma do?

Choose what Basma should do:

① Tell the others to wash their hands.

② Eat without washing her hands.

③ Wash her hands and not bother to say anything to the others.

or...

④ Can you think of something else?

Should they cut the pretty flowers?

Flower cutters

It's springtime and the daffodils in the garden pots are flowering.

Emma and Peter want to cut the flowers and take them in to the classroom. Basma wants to leave them to make the garden pretty.

What should the children do?

Choose what the children should do:

1. Cut all of the flowers off.

2. Leave the flowers in the garden.

3. Go and buy some flowers for the classroom.

or...

4. Can you think of something else?

19

Fariq is fed up with his watering duty.

I'm fed up with this

It is Fariq's turn to water the garden. But he doesn't want to do it.

"I'm fed up with having to do this every week," he says to Basma.

What should Basma do?

Choose what Basma should do:

① Do the watering for him.

② Tell him off for not helping out.

③ Find someone else to do the watering.

or...

④ Can you think of something else?

The holidays approach. Who will water the flowers?

A holiday problem

It's holiday time and everyone will be away from school for three weeks.

Basma and her friends normally water the plants when there is a dry spell.

What should Basma do?

Choose what Basma should do:

① Hope that it will rain from time to time.

② Come back to school and water the plants each week.

③ Ask the caretaker to water the plants.

or...

④ Can you think of something else?

23

Basma has learned these things:

- That a school garden needs a team of people.

- That everyone in a team has to pull their weight.

- That everyone in a team can help to decide what is to be done.

- That everyone needs to feel wanted.

Have you thought of helping make a school garden?

Do you know how to be part of a team?

Do you know how to help lead a team?

24